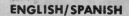

ENGLISH/SPANISH

What Do I Do?

Story: NORMA SIMON

Pictures: JOE LASKER

Albert Whitman & Company • Morton Grove, Illinois

Other Books Written by Norma Simon
And Illustrated by Joe Lasker
ALL KINDS OF FAMILIES
HOW DO I FEEL?
WHAT DO I SAY?
WHAT DO I SAY? *English/Spanish Edition*

Standard Book Number 8075-8823-7
Library of Congress Card Number 74-79544
Text © 1969 by Norma Simon; Illustrations © 1969 by Joe Lasker.
Published in 1969 by Albert Whitman & Company,
6340 Oakton Street, Morton Grove, Illinois 60053.
Published simultaneously in Canada by
General Publishing, Limited, Toronto.
Printed in the United States of America.
12   11   10   9   8   7   6

A Note About This Book ...

The little girl in this book is Consuelo, a Puerto Rican child whose home is in a city housing project.

Like little girls everywhere, Consuelo is striving to grow and feel competent and comfortable in her world. The women she knows are capable and motherly, and she imitates them. But like all youngsters she also enjoys play, drawing pictures, and having fun. Her experiences are ones any girl or boy can share. When Consuelo asks "What do I do?" a child makes this book his own by supplying the answer.

At home Consuelo is more likely to speak Spanish than English. If at school she has a bilingual teacher, she is fortunate. But even if the teacher speaks Spanish, Consuelo and her friends rarely see books with Spanish as well as English words. This English/Spanish edition of WHAT DO I DO? is planned to meet this need.

Please note that the English and Spanish are often, but not always, direct translations of each other. Some English idioms are given in Spanish words that convey a similar meaning but are not word-for-word translations. In both languages the speech is child-like and colloquial.

The bilingual book permits a choice of language to fit a child's ability. It can also be used to introduce a second language — English phrases to the Spanish-speaking child or Spanish to the English user. But no matter what the language, the illustrations for this book and their warmth help overcome word barriers.

NORMA SIMON

All gone!

¡Se acabó!

Baby wants more.

La nena quiere más.

What do I do?
¿Qué hago?

I run to get more milk.
Corro a buscar más leche.

No more milk.
No hay más leche.

Oh, oh!
¡Oh! ¡Oh!

What do I do?
¿Qué hago?

Can I help?
¿Te puedo ayudar?

Can I have money?
¿Me dás dinero?

I go to the store.
Voy a la tienda.

I find the milk.
Encuentro la leche.

What do I do?
¿Qué hago?

I put the milk down.
Coloco la leche.

What do I do?
¿Qué hago?

I pay the man.
Le pago al hombre.

Here, Baby!
¡Toma, Bebé!

Big Brother says,
"It's time to go."

Mi hermano mayor dice,
"Es hora de irnos."

What do we do?

¿Qué hacemos?

We go to school.
Vamos a la escuela.

Mrs. Wood says, "Here's Joe. He's new."
La Señora Wood dice, "Este es Joe. El es nuevo aquí."

What do I do?
¿Qué hago?

I tell him my name.
Le digo mi nombre.

"I'm Consuelo."
"Me llamo Consuelo."

Joe wants my wagon.
Joe quiere mi carro.

What do I do?
¿Qué hago?

I say, "Let's take turns."
Yo digo, "Vamos a turnarnos."

Joe makes the wagon go.
Joe echa andar el carro.

I have a cold.
Yo tengo catarro.

What do I do?
¿Qué hago?

I wipe my nose.
Me limpio la nariz.

Here are paper and crayons.
Aquí hay papel y creyones.

What do I do?   I make a picture.
¿Qué hago?   Yo pinto un cuadro.

Time to go home!
¡Es hora de irnos!

I take my picture.
Me llevo mi cuadro.

What do I do?

¿Qué hago?

I hang my picture on the wall.
Yo cuelgo mi cuadro en la pared.

Everybody likes my picture.
A todos les gusta mi cuadro.

What do I do?
¿Qué hago?

I smile.

Me sonrío.

I want to play.
Quiero jugar.

I can't find my doll.
No encuentro mi muñeca.

What do I do?
¿Qué hago?

I look in my drawer.
Miro dentro de mi gaveta.

I bang my finger!
¡Me golpeo mi dedo!

What do I do?
¿Qué hago?

Help!
  ¡Ayúdenme!

I run cold water on my finger.
  Me echo agua fría.

Aaaaah!
  ¡Aaaaah!

Baby wants to go out.
La nena quiere salir.

What do I do?
¿Qué hago?

I take her for a walk.
La llevo a pasear.

It's suppertime.
Es hora de comer.

What do I do?
¿Qué hago?

I set the table.
Pongo la mesa.

I spill my milk.   What do I do?
Se me derramó mi leche.   ¿Qué hago?

I'm sorry.   I clean it up.
Lo siento.   Lo limpio.

Everybody is busy.
Todos están ocupados.

What do I do?
¿Qué hago?

I look at TV.
Miro la televisión.

My face is washed.
Me lavé la cara.

My teeth are brushed.
Me lavé los dientes.

What do I do?
¿Qué hago?

I get into my pajamas.
Me pongo mis pijamas.

I put out the light.
Apago la luz.

Then what do I do?
¿Qué hago ahora?

I go to sleep.
Me acuesto a dormir.